The
Mermaid
of
Hilton Head

Written &
Illustrated by:

Nina Leipold

Palmetto Publishing Group, LLC
www.PalmettoPublishingGroup.com

The Mermaid of Hilton Head
Copyright ©2016 Nina Leipold
www.MermaidOfHiltonHead.com

ISBN-13: 978-1-944313-38-8
ISBN-10: 1-944313-38-9

Dedicated to George Trovato

The Mermaid of Hilton Head loves living in the waters around Hilton Head Island. She swims freely and frolics with her ocean friends all day long!

However, she didn't always live here. . .

1

The Mermaid of Hilton Head was at one time nomadic, which means she traveled with her mermaid pod along the East Coast, from Florida to the Outer Banks.

2

She and her pod would befriend manatees, dolphins, whales, sharks, and sea turtles along the way. They were always careful not to be seen by humans because the mermaids were very shy.

Every summer when her pod passed Hilton Head Island, the mermaid would notice huge, majestic three-hundred-fifty-pound sea turtles crawling onto the beaches.

4

Then they would turn around and go back to the ocean.

5

She thought this was odd and wondered why they would come onto land just to turn right around and go home.

The other mermaids didn't know either, but they didn't seem to care as much as she did.

The turtles weren't catching food. They weren't sleeping. They weren't meeting up with other turtles.

She simply couldn't figure out why they'd waste all that energy for no apparent reason, so she set out to investigate!

While her pod kept moving along, the Mermaid of Hilton Head stayed behind, and every night she would swim alongside boats and listen to the sailors' conversations.

She had to be ever so quiet so they wouldn't see her. For weeks on end, she followed the boats, putting herself in danger so she could listen to the sailors.

Finally, one night she overheard them
talking about the sea turtles.

The sailors seemed to think that the sea turtles went onto land at night to lay their eggs and then they would become scared by the lights on land and return to the ocean. The sailors referred to this as a "false crawl."

This made sense to the mermaid because Hilton Head Island was the only place she'd seen this happen in such great numbers-and the only place along her pod's route that had so many lights and so much beach activity.

The baby turtles also became confused by the lights after they hatched, and they would venture inland instead of following the moonlight to the ocean.

15

The mermaid knew no one else was going to help the turtles.

It was up to her to do something to make the sea turtles feel more comfortable so they would lay their eggs and so the babies could find their way home after hatching.

The next night, the mermaid came across
a sea turtle swimming toward shore.

Like every other night, there were a lot of lights on land. This was the mermaid's chance to take action and save the turtles!

19

She thought and she thought about what to do, and she came up with an idea. She did something brave-something no other mermaid had ever done before.

She hurried closer to the beach and started calling out:
"Lights out! Lights out!"

She knew the humans might see her, but it was a chance
she was willing to take to save the turtles.

The mermaid became disappointed when the lights onshore didn't turn off. She shouted out again, even louder this time:

"Lights out! Lights out!"

And then it happened. The lights onshore began to disappear, and soon the beach was lit only by moonlight.

The mermaid couldn't believe it. Her plan was working!

The turtle reached land minutes later,
just like before, except this time she crawled the
whole way to the sand dunes and laid her eggs.

26

When she returned to the ocean,
she appeared to be much happier
and more relaxed.

This made the mermaid's heart fill with joy.

Such a simple solution like turning off the lights could help save the turtles!

Ever since, the Mermaid of Hilton Head has dedicated her life to saving sea turtles. With such an easy solution, how could she feel right doing anything else?

Now, every night around ten o'clock, if you listen closely, you'll hear the mermaid calling out a reminder for everyone onshore to turn off their lights.

31

Once all the lights are out, the mermaid is able to relax and
retreats to a safe spot to go to sleep.

The Mermaid of Hilton Head has come to love living in the waters surrounding Hilton Head Island.

She has become good friends with the local dolphins,
Stu, Cheerio, and Nick (just to name a few).

And nothing brings the Mermaid of Hilton Head more joy than calling out and watching the lights go out every night so she can help save the sea turtles.

36

About the Author

Nina Leipold, originally from Pennsylvania, now lives on Hilton Head Island in South Carolina. Aquatic conservation is extremely important to her; she's a former dolphin trainer and is working toward her captain's license. Along with being a breath-trained freediver, Leipold is a certified SCUBA diver.

Leipold was inspired to write her first children's book, *Sammy the Sand Dollar*, after seeing so many people unknowingly kill sand dollars by removing them from the ocean for home decorating purposes. Through her first book and *The Mermaid of Hilton Head*, Leipold hopes to educate children on the importance of nature conservation.

What You Can Do to Help
Hilton Head Stay Wild

- If you see injured wildlife such as birds, turtles, dolphins, alligators, or other land mammals, please do not harass or touch them. Instead, report them by calling the South Carolina Department of Natural Resources (SCDNR) at 1-800-922-5431, or call Hilton Head's Beach Patrol at 1-843-785-3494.

- It is against the law to feed dolphins or alligators. It's also illegal to harass any wildlife, which includes taking live sand dollars and starfish from their ocean homes. If you see someone do any of these things, please report it to Hilton Head's Beach Patrol at 1-843-785-3494.

- To report a dead or injured turtle, call SCDNR (24/7) at 1-800-922-5431.

- To report light violations (e.g., if beachfront properties have their lights on after 10:00 p.m.), call 1-843-341-4642.

- Join the exclusive membership group called the Mermaid Pod to learn about conservation and events aimed at giving back. 10 percent of the cost of the pod membership is donated to the Sea Turtle Hospital in the South Carolina Aquarium. To learn more about the pod, visit our website at www.MermaidofHiltonHead.com.

CPSIA information can be obtained at www.ICGtesting.com
Printed in the USA
BVIW12n0102220118
505948BV00002B/33